LONGMAN CLASSICS

P9-DHT-534

The Mysterious Island

Jules Verne

Simplified by D K Swan
Illustrated by Ivan Lapper

Longman

Longman Group Limited,
Edinburgh Gate, Harlow,
Essex CM20 2JE, England
and Associated Companies throughout the world.

This simplified edition © Longman Group UK Limited 1988

First published 1988
Eighth impression 1996

ISBN 0-582-54143-3

Set in 12/14 point Linotron 202 Versailles
Printed in China
LAPT/08

Acknowledgements

The cover background is a wallpaper design called NUAGE,
courtesy of Osborne and little plc.

Stage 2: 900 word vocabulary

Please look under *New words* at the back of this book
for explanations of words outside this stage.

Contents

Introduction

1	In the balloon	1
2	The island	4
3	Cyrus Smith is found	6
4	Life on the island	9
5	The box	11
6	The rock wall	12
7	Finding the cave	14
8	"Cave House"	18
9	Pirates!	22
10	Torpedo!	27
11	The mysterious friend	29
12	Down the hole	31
13	Captain Nemo	33
14	Leaving the island	37

Questions	39
New words	42

Introduction

The writer Jules Verne was born at Nantes, in the west of France, in 1828. Dates are quite important in this Introduction. Jules Verne's stories told the readers about very many things that were going to be used or discovered or invented in the future. For example, there is a big submarine in *The Mysterious Island*, which Jules Verne wrote in 1874. There *were* submarines at that time. Indeed, the French had a submarine called the *Nautilus* in 1801. It carried three men, and they turned its propeller by hand. The appearance of a power-driven submarine like the one in this book had to wait until the development of the internal combustion (petrol) engine in 1885. The electric lights in the submarine might have been like those that Edison developed in 1879.

Jules Verne studied law, but he began writing plays for the stage. In 1862 he produced the first novel of the kind he is best known for today. It was *Cinq semaines en ballon* (*Five Weeks in a Balloon*). It showed that Jules Verne could make imaginary journeys exciting. And it was the first of the novels that have given Verne the name of the "father of science fiction". It was an immediate success in France. People in other countries heard about it, and Verne's French novel was translated – into English, for example, in 1869.

Other science fiction novels followed. Here are just four of them:

1864 *Voyage to the Centre of the Earth*

1865 *From the Earth to the Moon* – in the story the journey took 97 hours 20 minutes.

1869 *Twenty Thousand Leagues under the Sea* – in which Jules Verne introduced the devilish Captain Nemo in his submarine, the *Nautilus*. You will meet Captain Nemo again in this book.

1873 *Round the World in Eighty Days* – with plenty of laughter added to the adventure and scientific discovery. By this time, there was no delay: the novel appeared in English and other languages in the same year 1873.

The science fiction stories of Jules Verne are still popular. Readers have certainly met one or more of them in film or on television. The success of his books made it possible for him to buy a fishing-boat on which he sailed and wrote. As he became more successful, he bought bigger boats and sailed longer distances. All the time, the books poured from his pen.

It was only when he lost his eyesight in 1902 that Jules Verne stopped writing and sailing. He died in 1905.

In the balloon

Chapter 1
In the balloon

You have heard about the hurricane of March 1865. That great storm destroyed cities and forests and ships in many parts of the world.

When the wind began – quite suddenly – there were four men, a boy, and a dog high in the air in the basket of a balloon. They were escaping from the town of Richmond, Virginia, where the men had been prisoners of war.

The hurricane caught the balloon and carried it far over the Pacific Ocean. The balloon travelled very fast – sometimes at about one hundred and sixty kilometres an hour – over that great sea.

At last, the wind became rather less strong. But it had made holes in the balloon, and the balloon began to fall towards the sea.

"Throw out some sand!"

"That's the last bag of sand."

"And are we going up again?"

"No!"

"Look! We are getting near the sea!"

"Yes. I can hear the waves. They are huge waves! What can we do?"

"Throw out everything!"

The voice that gave the orders was strong and without fear. It was the voice of Cyrus Smith.

They threw out everything that had weight:

guns, food, water, money. The balloon began to rise. For two hours it travelled through the air towards the south. But it was getting nearer to the water all the time.

There was no land in sight – just the sea with its frightening great waves.

"We must cut off the basket," said Cyrus Smith. "Climb up into the net. And let the basket fall into the water."

It was the only way to keep the balloon from dropping among the white wave tops. The four men and the boy climbed up into the net and pulled the dog up beside them. Then the ropes were cut, the basket fell away, and the balloon climbed once more.

"Land!" one of the men suddenly called out. It was Pencroft. He was a sailor, and his eyes were good. The others looked where he was pointing, and they could just see hills in the distance. The land was far away, and the balloon was coming down again.

The giant waves seemed to reach up to tear them from the net.

Suddenly Cyrus Smith was in the sea!

Did the sea pull him from the net, or did he jump to give the others a chance? Certainly the balloon, free from his weight, rose again. Top, the dog, saw his master in the water and jumped after him.

Before long, the balloon fell again, but this time it was over a sandy shore. The three men and the boy jumped down to the ground before the wind tore the balloon back into the sky.

They ran back to the water's edge.

"Perhaps Cyrus Smith is trying to swim here. We must be ready to save him." One man spoke for them all. He was Gideon Spillet, a reporter for the *New York Herald*.

The sailor, Pencroft, thought the same, but he also saw that they were on a very small island. It was near to a very much bigger piece of land.

"If Cyrus Smith is swimming," Pencroft said, "the sea will carry him to the coast of the big island. We must look for him there. Besides, there is no water here, and there are no trees. We can't stay here."

Nab, the third man, had already decided. He threw himself into the water and started to swim to the big island. He was Cyrus Smith's servant, and he loved his master more than he loved his own life.

Chapter 2
The island

The others could all swim, but not so well as Nab. By the time they were on the bigger island, Nab had disappeared. He had gone to look for Cyrus Smith.

They looked round them.

"There seem to be plenty of trees," said Spillet. "And I saw hills, so there are probably streams with fresh water coming down from them. I want to climb a hill and look at the island. We must know if there are people and houses anywhere. Will you two walk along the shore and look for food and water? We'll meet again here before the sun goes down."

Pencroft and Herbert, the boy, walked along the beach to the south. They had not gone far when Pencroft said: "Those rocks by the edge of the water will make a very good house for us. And there's a little stream just beyond them. That will bring fresh water. There'll be food on the rocks too."

"Food?" said Herbert. "I can see rocks for a house and a stream for water, but where's the food?"

"It'll be on the rocks. I've been round the world, you know, and there are always shellfish on rocks like those."

Herbert saw another difficulty.

4

"We can't eat these shellfish without cooking them, and we haven't got a fire."

The sailor felt in his pockets, but his box of matches had gone.

"Perhaps the others have some matches," he said. "Let's go and get wood for a fire and the branches of trees for a roof and a door to finish our rock house."

They went among the trees. Herbert found some eggs and Pencroft found dead wood for a fire and the best branches for the house. They took all these things to the rock, and then it was time to meet Spillet.

The reporter had met Nab, and they came to the meeting place together. But it was clear that they had had no success in looking for Cyrus Smith. Spillet looked very tired, and Nab's eyes were red with weeping.

"I went to the top of the highest hill in this part of the island," said Spillet. "I couldn't see any houses or people. And neither Nab nor I have been able to find anything to show that Cyrus Smith or his dog reached the island."

Chapter 3
Cyrus Smith is found

Spillet found one match in his pocket.

"We can light a fire with this if we are very careful," Pencroft said. "But we must never let the fire go out."

They had a meal of birds' eggs and shellfish. Then most of them tried to sleep.

Spillet had a notebook in his pocket. Before he slept, he made notes like a good reporter: the storm, the arrival at the island, the unsuccessful search for Cyrus Smith, even the fire and the food and the rock house.

Pencroft woke every hour and put wood on the fire. Nab couldn't sleep, or he didn't want to. He walked up and down the beach all night. Only young Herbert slept well.

It was still night when Nab came to the door of the rock house.

"Top's here!" he said.

Top looked at the men and the boy. He barked loudly. Then he ran out of the rock house, came back and barked again, ran out again.

"Top wants us to follow him," said Nab. "Perhaps he'll lead us to my master. Let's go!"

"How did the dog find us?" Spillet wondered. "It's most surprising. He had never been to our part of the shore, but he seems to have come straight to us. He isn't even tired."

They hurried after the dog. The sun came up, and still Top led them on. About five kilometres along the shore, the dog turned away from the sea and led them towards some hills.

"He's going into that cave!" said Pencroft.

The cave was in the side of a hill. It was safely above the height of any waves coming in from the sea, even in the strongest wind.

They all ran into the cave.

Cyrus Smith was there. He was lying on soft sand, but his eyes were closed, and he was not moving.

"Oh!" cried Nab. "He's dead!"

Spillet put his ear to Smith's chest and held up his hand to ask for silence.

"No," he said, "he isn't dead. But he's only just alive."

They forced some water into Smith's mouth, then Spillet listened again to his heart.

"It's beating more strongly," he said. "I think he's going to be all right."

About three hours later, Cyrus Smith was able to talk.

"Where am I?" he asked. His voice was very weak.

"I think we're on an island," Spillet said. And they told Smith what they had found out about the island.

"How did I get into this place?" Smith asked when he was stronger. "I remember swimming with Top towards the land, and I remember that a great wave threw me up on the shore. But I don't remember anything else. How far am I from the sea?"

"At least a kilometre," said Pencroft.

"Then somebody carried me."

"It wasn't one of us," said Spillet. "And we haven't seen anyone else on the island. You must have walked here."

"That's not possible. I was far too weak."

With Pencroft and Nab holding him up, Cyrus Smith went to the mouth of the cave and looked at the ground. There was one place where the ground was wet, and there were the clear marks of a man's feet. None of the others had stepped there.

"They aren't the marks of my feet," said Cyrus Smith. "They're the marks of shoes, and I'm not wearing shoes. My shoes are in the sea!"

"It's a mystery," said Spillet. And that is what he wrote in his notebook when, at last, they had carried Smith back to the rock house.

Cyrus Smith was too weak to eat more than one of Herbert's eggs that night. But the next day he was much stronger.

"What is there to eat?" he asked.

"Shellfish or eggs," answered Pencroft.

"What kind of eggs?"

"I think they're the eggs of a kind of duck," Herbert said. "But I'm not sure. I found them on the ground – more than twenty of them – all together in one place."

Chapter 4
Life on the island

"If there are eggs," said Cyrus Smith, "there must be the birds that laid them. So that is one more thing that we can eat – ducks or birds of that kind. With the fruit that we are sure to find on the trees."

"How are we going to catch or kill the birds?" asked Herbert. "We threw the guns out of the basket when the balloon was falling. I tried throwing stones at some birds yesterday, but I couldn't hit them."

"We'll have to make bows and arrows," Spillet said.

Pencroft knew, and found, the right kind of wood for bows, and he began to shape them with his knife. It was a sailor's knife that he always carried, and they had good reason to be glad that he still had it. The knife was also useful for shaping arrows.

Then the colonists (as the four men and the boy had decided to call themselves) had to learn how to use the bows and arrows. Spillet and Herbert soon showed that they were going to be good bowmen. Before long, they were bringing in a supply of wild ducks and other birds.

At first the colonists cooked their food over or under the fire. But Nab knew how to make pots. He found the right kind of clay in the sides of a little river, and soon they were able to cook their food in large and small pots.

"We're doing very well," said Spillet, "but there are very many things that we need. I could make a very long list of the tools and other things that would make life easier." And he named some of the things that would be on his list.

Two days later, the colonists went to see what there was to the south of the rock house. They had not gone far when Pencroft called out:

"Look! What's that?"

On the beach there was a very big box.

"I suppose it is from a ship," said Cyrus Smith, "but it looks very heavy. Why didn't it go to the bottom?"

"I think I know," Pencroft said. He pointed to some strong-looking material on the sand round the box. "The box has had air bags round it – bags full of air. They would keep it on top of the water. I wonder what there is inside."

He picked up a heavy piece of rock to break the lock. But Cyrus Smith stopped him.

"Don't break the box," said Smith. "It could be very useful. Locks of this kind can be opened by turning the parts to the right number. Let me see if I can find the number by feeling."

The colonists watched while Cyrus Smith's fingers moved the parts of the lock. At last it opened, and Pencroft and Nab raised the top.

The box was quite dry inside, and full.

Chapter 5
The box

"This is most surprising," Spillet said. "It's as if somebody heard my list of things we need."

There were tools and instruments of different kinds: knives, axes, hammers, nails, things for digging, sewing and measuring, a lot of rope, matches, and a lot of fishing things.

There were weapons: guns, gunpowder and shot, swords.

There were things for making shoes, as well as lengths of cloth, and twenty shirts.

Things for cooking and eating, metal pots and pans, table knives, forks and spoons.

"There's even paper and things for writing," said Spillet happily. "There's everything we need!"

"Nearly everything," Pencroft said.

"Oh? What else could we want?" Herbert asked.

"Just a little tobacco for my pipe."

"We'll look for a plant that you can dry and smoke," said Cyrus Smith. "We'll look for it tomorrow, because I think we ought to start again on our journey to the south. There are things I don't understand here. But first we'll bring the box itself into the rock house."

That was hard work, but at last they had the big box safely inside the house.

Chapter 6
The rock wall

In the morning the colonists took food, weapons, and a few tools and instruments, and started again along the beach towards the south. It was not necessary for one of them to stay behind. Since the arrival of the big box, they had had no difficulty in lighting a fire. The fire in the rock house could go out for the first time. They left everything else in the big box.

Not very far from the rock house, the beach became narrower. On the land side, there were some forest trees, and then a high wall of rock rose straight up to a height of about fifty metres.

"I saw this rock wall from the top of a hill on our first day on the island," said Spillet. "It *is* like a wall, only about half a kilometre thick. And on the other side of it there is a big lake. The water in the lake comes down in a river from the mountain on the other side."

"And where does it go out?" Cyrus Smith asked.

"Must it go out?"

"Yes," said Smith. "If it comes into the lake as a river, the water must go out somewhere. If it didn't, the lake would get fuller and fuller ... Let's go and see what happens to the water."

They went round the end of the rock wall. It was a very difficult journey, but at last they came to the side of the lake. Pencroft and Nab tried to catch fish in the lake, but there seemed to be very few.

The colonists slept beside the lake and then moved round behind the rock wall.

"The lake water seems to be flowing this way," said Herbert, pointing towards some thick forest at the foot of the rock wall.

Cyrus Smith led the way. The noise of falling water grew louder and louder. Suddenly they came to an opening in the trees. In front of them was a river flowing out of the lake. It flowed almost to the rock wall – and then, the bottom of the river ended sharply, and the water fell over the edge and out of sight.

Cyrus Smith stood and looked round him for some time. Then he pointed to a big hole in the rock wall, about ten metres above the place where they were standing.

"That's the way the water of the lake used to flow out," he said. "Now it seems to have found a new way. Perhaps it comes out under the sea, because we didn't see any river on the other side of the rock wall. But I want to see the way it flowed before."

The colonists looked at the hole in the rock.

"We'll need light if we are going in there," said Pencroft. "Nab and I will find the right wood for torches."

Chapter 7
Finding the cave

The hole in the rock wall above the waterfall was about six metres wide, but it was only about a metre high. It was not easy to get through it, but Nab and Pencroft made it a little higher.

Cyrus Smith took a torch and led the way inside. After the low entrance there was a passage about two metres high. It went slowly down. The rock floor had been worn by water, and the colonists had to walk carefully.

"We must have a rope, like mountain climbers," Smith decided. "Then if someone falls down a hole, the others can hold him."

The danger of falling was not great. Top, the clever dog, went first. They were sure he would warn them of any danger.

After a time, the passage led into a long cave, and they were able to move rather faster.

Cyrus Smith was watching an instrument that he had found in the big box.

"We aren't going in a straight line, as you can see," he said, "but the general line is towards the sea."

The passage became narrower again – about four metres wide and four metres high.

They came round a bend in the passage – and stopped. They were at the opening of a huge cave.

Pencroft and Nab waved their torches about, to make their light brighter. Cyrus Smith and Spillet stood ready with their weapons. But there was nothing to see in the great cave. At the far end there was some light.

"We'll move towards that light," said Smith. "I think it comes from the side of the rock wall nearest to the sea. But we must be careful. There may be a place where the water used to fall. It must certainly have run out to the sea. Top, go in front of us."

Top ran towards the far end of the huge cave. Before he reached it, he stopped and barked loudly.

Cyrus Smith and the other colonists moved carefully towards the dog. Their torches lit up a big opening in the floor of the cave. It went straight down, like a huge well. The torches could not show the bottom, so Smith broke off a branch of the torch wood. He lit it and threw it down the opening. As it fell, he counted. After a time, they heard the sound as the light was put out by water.

"So this hole ends in water," Cyrus Smith said. "That must be at sea level. My counting shows that we are about thirty metres above sea level."

"How far away is the sea?" asked Spillet.

"I think the light comes from the rock wall above the shore," said Smith. "Let's find our way round this hole and go on."

The colonists find the hole in the cave floor

They found that the light did come from small cracks in the rock.

"The rock seems to be least thick at this place," said Pencroft, pointing to one of the cracks. "I could make the crack wider."

"Try," said Cyrus Smith.

Using one of the tools that had come from the big box, Pencroft attacked the rock beside the crack. When he was tired, Nab worked at the crack. Then Spillet.

Suddenly a big piece of rock fell away from the crack. The nearest part of the cave was filled with light. They looked round them. It was a huge space, clean and dry. At one side, a small stream gave a supply of clean fresh water.

"We ought to make some more windows like the one Mr Spillet has just made," said Herbert. "Then we could have a wonderful house here."

"The torches won't last much longer," said Pencroft, "and we need them to find our way back through the passages to the lake."

The last torch went out just after the colonists reached the opening near the lake.

"We'll have to spend another night beside the lake," Cyrus Smith said.

It was not a good night. A very bad storm blew up.

"I'm very glad we have the great wall to save us from the worst of the storm," Spillet said.

Chapter 8
"Cave House"

The colonists had a difficult journey back to the shore. Trees had been blown down, the ground was very wet, and the streams were swollen.

At last they came in sight of the sea. Although the wind was much less, there were huge waves rolling in to the beach.

"The waves have been right up the shore as far as the trees," said Cyrus Smith. "I wonder what has happened at the rock house."

The colonists reached the rock house in the afternoon. The sea had broken down the roof and door, and the sleeping places and Pencroft's fireplace had been destroyed. Only the big box was all right. The water had washed over it, and even moved it a little, but it was dry inside. Not a drop of water had found its way in.

"We'll have to move our home higher up," said Cyrus Smith.

"To the great cave?" Herbert asked.

"That's possible," said Smith, "if ..."

"If what?" Pencroft wanted to know.

Cyrus Smith smiled. "I was thinking," he said. "We couldn't use the long dark passages to reach the big cave every time. We would have to find another way in."

Spillet said, "Isn't there a way up from this side – the shore side?"

"I looked at it from this side," Smith answered. "The hole we made is about twenty-five metres up the rock wall above the ground." He turned to the sailor. "Pencroft, is it possible to make a rope ladder twenty-five metres long?"

"Yes," said Pencroft. "But the wind could make it dangerous. The rock wall has a kind of shelf, half-way up. So we could make two shorter ladders."

"Have we got enough rope?" Spillet asked.

"I know how to make rope," the sailor said. "And there's plenty of material for rope-making in the forest."

So the colonists spent a week moving into their new home. "Cave House", they called it. They broke open some more windows. Pencroft and Spillet made ropes and set rope ladders up the rock wall. Herbert and Nab made beds, chairs and tables out of wood that they pulled up by ropes. Cyrus Smith prepared places for cooking, eating, bathing and sleeping.

If the colonists had any problems, Cyrus Smith found the answers – answers like:

"We must be able to pull the rope ladders up. Then no enemy could reach us."

"We must have a food store. There may be days when we can't get fruit or other food from the forest."

"We must find a tree that gives oil for our lamps."

While the work was going on, the colonists learnt a lot about each other.

Young Herbert did very well. Things that he made were well planned and carefully built. He had never used tools before, but when Pencroft or Nab showed him how to use them, he learnt quickly.

Pencroft thought that Cyrus Smith was wonderful. He was not afraid of their leader, but he listened carefully when Smith talked. The sailor liked talking, himself. He told a lot of stories about his life as a seaman, and some of the stories may not have been entirely true. Herbert and Nab enjoyed them. Smith and Spillet let him talk and tell his stories. They knew he was a good and brave man, and the things he had learnt at sea were very often useful to the colonists.

Nab was just Nab, brave, always ready to help, willing to do anything – even to die – for Cyrus Smith. Nab and Pencroft were soon very good friends. There was one difference between them. When Pencroft showed surprise at Smith's great powers, Nab found them quite natural and was never surprised. "Of course" his master was wonderful.

Pencroft was surprised at Gideon Spillet too. "A writer," the sailor thought, "a newspaper reporter, but he doesn't only understand things, he can *do* things too. He can use his hands as well as his head!"

The colonists in their new home

Chapter 9
Pirates!

One day, Cyrus Smith said, "We must set a watch for ships."

"We have been watching," said Spillet.

"Yes. But not all the time. We ought to have somebody at one of the Cave House windows all the time."

That is how it happened that Herbert, who was on watch at the window one afternoon, called out: "A ship! A ship!"

Cyrus Smith had a plan to call the attention of any passing ship. But this ship was still too far away.

"Is it coming towards us?" he asked.

"I'm not sure yet," said Pencroft.

They continued to watch. The ship came nearer, but the daylight was ending, and at the same time the wind was less strong.

"I can see the ship's flag," Pencroft said, "but it is hanging down. It isn't American, or British, or French——"

Just then, the wind blew for a moment, and he saw the flag clearly. "The black flag!"

All kinds of thoughts passed through Cyrus Smith's mind. A pirate ship! What did it want in that part of the Pacific? Had it come to hide stolen goods on the island? Did the pirates want a safe place for times of storm?

"Listen, my friends," he said. "Perhaps they are only looking at this island. Perhaps they won't land here. But we mustn't let them see that there are people here. Pull up the rope ladders, and pull the branches over the windows."

They had already prepared branches to hide the Cave House windows if it was necessary.

The ship came in towards the shore. The colonists could only wait. Night fell.

"They're staying here," said Pencroft, as they heard the anchor going down. "They'll come to the shore in their small boats in the morning."

"Let's hope they have only come for water," Cyrus Smith said. "Then they might sail away again and never know about us."

Pencroft spoke. "I think I'll go and find out."

"How?" asked Herbert.

"I can swim."

They let the rope ladders down, and Pencroft was soon on the shore. He swam strongly out to where he saw the ship's lights. Then, as he came near the ship, he turned on his side and swam silently. He reached the ship, found the anchor rope, and rested with his hand on it.

After a time, he climbed carefully up the rope to just below the level of the ship's rail.

Some men were talking.

"It's a good ship, this."

"Yes, and it was easy getting it. I'm sorry we had to kill the women and children as well as the men."

"But it's safer like that."

"Oh, yes! The captain knows!"

"Good old Bob Harvey!"

Pencroft knew that name! Bob Harvey was the most dangerous pirate in the Pacific Ocean – in the world, perhaps. He and his men had escaped from a prison in Australia.

The men were drinking and talking in loud voices. They were pleased with themselves, with the ship and with their heartless captain. Pencroft heard them laughing as they talked about what they had done to women and children on ships and on peaceful Pacific islands.

"But what can we do?" he asked himself. "I must know how many pirates there are, and what weapons they have."

He waited until the men were asleep. Then he climbed on to the darkened ship. There were about fifty men, he thought, and they had plenty of guns. The ship had four big guns that could reach the rock wall from where they were anchored.

There was nothing more that he could do, and he swam back to the shore.

In Cave House, Pencroft told his story. He ended by saying, "Five of us against fifty of them! Do you think we have a chance, Mr Smith?"

"Yes," said Cyrus Smith.

The rest of the night passed without trouble. Next morning, they saw men moving around

Pencroft reaches the pirates' ship

on the ship. The anchor was pulled up, sails were set, and the ship began to move closer to the shore. When it was quite near, the watchers heard the sound of a big gun. The pirates were shooting at the rocks and trees along the shore.

"They haven't seen anything," said Spillet, "but they are making sure that there is no danger before they send out the small boats."

As he spoke, one of the shots came high up the rock wall.

"I don't think Bob Harvey has seen anything," said Cyrus Smith. "That was a mistake."

But the wind of the explosion tore away some of the branches that hid one of the Cave House windows.

"That's bad," said Pencroft. "Bob Harvey isn't a fool. He'll see the opening, and we can expect more shots up here."

"Yes," said Smith. "Stand away from the windows. I hoped this wouldn't happen. The pirates can't reach us here, but they can keep us in Cave House like prisoners."

As he was speaking, there was the noise of an explosion from outside. It was followed by fearful cries.

Cyrus Smith and the other colonists ran to one of the windows.

The ship had been lifted into the air on a great mass of water. As it fell back again, they saw that it had been torn into two parts. In less than ten seconds, it had gone to the bottom!

Chapter 10
Torpedo!

"Quick!" said Cyrus Smith. "Down to the shore, everybody! Take your guns with you. We must be sure that none of the pirates are alive and a danger to us."

There was nothing of the ship above the water, but they could see it, in two halves, lying on the bottom.

The ship was on its side, and most of the men were caught below by the explosion. There were not many bodies for the colonists to bury.

"We'll have to wait for low water before we can dive down to see what we can save," said Pencroft. "I want to know, too, why it exploded like that."

"And just at the right moment," added Spillet.

"What surprises me," said Herbert, "is that the explosion didn't break the ship into very many pieces. It seems to be just in halves."

"It surprises me too," said Cyrus Smith. "Perhaps we'll find the answer at low water."

"A mystery?" asked Spillet.

"Yes, perhaps."

A few hours later, the side of the ship began to appear above the water. Pencroft and Nab swam to it.

The bottom of the ship had been torn in two.

"If the ship's gunpowder had exploded," Pencroft thought, "the upper parts would have blown up. Here the upper parts aren't badly broken up. There are bad cracks, but they aren't from an explosion. It is the bottom that has suffered."

For a few days, it was possible to visit the ship at low water. The colonists found cases of clothes and shoes – part of the ship's load before the pirates took it. They found dry gunpowder and several kinds of food. And, to Pencroft's great joy, tobacco.

But then a storm came, and the ship broke up. Some parts of it came to the beach, but other parts were washed into deep water.

"Now we won't know the answer to one question," said Cyrus Smith. "What really happened to the ship? You, Pencroft, are sure it didn't hit a rock?"

"Quite sure, Mr Smith. There aren't any rocks there. And some of us saw the ship go up on a great mass of water at the time of the explosion."

A few days after that, Nab was walking along the beach. He stopped and looked at a piece of metal. It had been part of a steel cylinder, but it had been bent and torn by an explosion. It was heavy, but he carried it to Cyrus Smith.

Smith looked at the remains of the cylinder.

He said, "This is what sent up the great mass of water and broke the ship's bottom. It is all that remains of a torpedo."

Chapter 11
The mysterious friend

"No," said Cyrus Smith. "I didn't make the torpedo, and I don't know where it came from. It does seem that there is at least one other person on this island. He or she helps us: saving me from the sea; supplying us with the things in the big box; and now destroying our enemies. So this mysterious person is a friend. I don't know why he or she hides from us, but I am sure it is a person. Top knows there is another person on the island, too. You have all seen and heard him barking at what seems to be nothing."

Nab spoke. "We won't see him until he wants to be seen."

The colonists knew he was right.

It was not long before they had another proof that they had a friend not far away.

Herbert was very ill. Cyrus Smith knew the illness and the medicine to give for it: sulphate of quinine. But there was no supply of quinine in the trees of the island. The colonists were very sad.

At about three o'clock in the morning, Nab was looking after Herbert. He moved away to mix a cool drink for the boy, but he ran back quickly when he heard Top barking. By the time Nab got to the boy's bed, Top had stopped barking. He seemed happy, and his nose was on the table, beside Herbert's bed.

On the table, Nab found a bottle. It had on it the words "Sulphate of Quinine". He quickly called Cyrus Smith.

Cyrus Smith smelt the medicine, tasted it, and then gave a small amount to the sick boy.

From that time on, Herbert's illness began to leave him.

"Our friend only comes to help us when we are in great danger," Cyrus Smith said.

Months passed. The mysterious helper did not appear.

Then one morning Top seemed excited, and Cyrus Smith was sure their friend had been in Cave House again.

There was a note on the table:

NOW *I* AM DYING. COME DOWN
THE BIG HOLE IN THE FLOOR.

Chapter 12
Down the hole

"We know there is water at the bottom of the hole. It's about thirty metres down. We need a rope at least sixty metres long."

"I'll go down first," said Pencroft. "If I need anything, I'll shout."

It was easy for the sailor to go down the rope. He took a torch with him in his mouth.

After a few minutes, they heard his voice: "I'm on a shelf of rock beside the water. I can't see far, but it seems to be another huge cave. Except for this shelf of rock, I think the bottom is all water."

Nab came down to help Pencroft. He brought another torch. While the others were coming down the ropes, Pencroft and Nab walked along the rock shelf.

"Look! A boat!" said Pencroft.

The boat was under the edge of the rock. It was tied to an iron ring in the rock. There were two oars under the seats.

When Cyrus Smith saw it, he said, "It's big enough for all of us. I think we are expected to get into it."

"Now where?" wondered Spillet when the colonists were all in the boat.

"I don't know," said Smith. He shouted: "Is anybody here?"

At once a powerful light lit up the cave. They saw that the floor of the cave was a lake, even bigger than they had thought.

And the light?

"Electric light!" said Cyrus Smith.

The light seemed to come from a long cigar-shaped object in the middle of the lake. It made no sound and no movement. It was about seventy-five metres long and it rose, in the middle, to about four metres above the water.

Smith gave an order, and the boat began to move towards this object.

The colonists' leader was standing up, staring hard at the thing in the water. Suddenly he took hold of Spillet's arm.

"It's him!" Smith said. And he said a name so quietly that only the reporter heard it. "It can't be anyone else!"

The name certainly meant something to Gideon Spillet.

"Him!" he said. "A man outside the law!"

Chapter 13
Captain Nemo

Pencroft brought the boat to the side of the thing and tied it there. The colonists climbed up a ladder to an entrance, which was open. Then Cyrus Smith led the way down steps to a passage. The whole of the inside was brightly lit by electricity.

At the end of the passage, Smith opened a heavy door. Beyond it there was a large room. It was full of fine things – pictures by great artists, wonderful jewels, beautiful furniture.

Lying on a richly cushioned seat was a man who seemed not to notice the arrival of the colonists.

To the great surprise of his friends, Cyrus Smith said in a loud voice: "Captain Nemo, you asked us to come. Here we are."

The man stood up, holding on to the back of his seat. It was clear that a slow illness was taking away his strength, but his voice was not weak when he said: "I did not give you my name, sir."

"I know you," Smith answered. "And I know this submarine, the *Nautilus*."

For a moment, Captain Nemo looked angry, but then he fell back on the cushions. "It doesn't matter. I'm dying. – I suppose you haven't heard anything good about me?"

"Does it matter what we have heard? What we *know* is that since we came to this island we have been helped by someone who is good."

"I have watched you," said the old man. "You are good people, and you help each other. I want to tell you my story.

"I am an Indian, Prince Dakkar. The great Indian leader, Tippu Sahib, was my uncle. When I was ten years old, my father sent me to Europe. I learnt everything the Europeans could teach me. I seemed, I suppose, to be just a rich student of the international world. But I had all the time a secret wish – a secret purpose. I wanted to learn everything so that I could destroy the British, who had conquered my country.

"I thought I saw my chance in 1857. The Indian soldiers of the British army rose against the British, and I became one of their leaders. We expected help from outside the country, but we didn't get any help. My men and I fought hard. I was wounded twenty times, and I wanted to die for my country, but death didn't come. When the last of the fighters for independence fell, I was forced to leave the country.

"Prince Dakkar, the freedom fighter, became Prince Dakkar the man of learning. But I found other men who had been forced to leave India, and they came with me on this submarine that I had planned and built. People have read about some of the things we did. But by the time I was

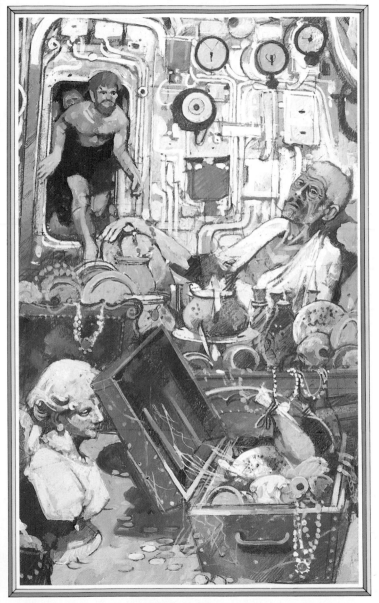

Captain Nemo

sixty years old, those friends of mine were nearly all dead. I brought the *Nautilus* here, and here I am waiting for death.

"The *Nautilus* will never go to sea again. The mouth of this cave fell in at the time of the great storm that brought you here."

Captain Nemo fell back against his cushions.

Cyrus Smith and Gideon Spillet talked quietly about ways of helping him to live. But they knew he was dying.

As if he had heard them, Captain Nemo said, "I'll be dead tomorrow. I want only one thing. When I am dead, I want you to leave the *Nautilus*. Take with you only that case of precious stones. They will make you all very rich one day, but I know you will do nothing but good with your riches. I want everything else to go with me when I die. When you go, get into the boat you came in. Then find two wheels, one at the back and one at the front of the submarine. Turn them. The water will come in, and *Nautilus* will go to the bottom. I want to be here in the submarine when that happens."

Chapter 14
Leaving the island

The colonists carried out Captain Nemo's wishes exactly. As the *Nautilus* went down, they reached the rock shelf. The electric light from the submarine lasted for long enough, even under the water, for them to find their ropes and start to climb them.

Their life went on. The boat from the submarine was very useful. Pencroft took it to pieces in the submarine cave and put it together again on the beach.

The boat helped them to get more and better fish. And they used it to get fruit and other supplies from other parts of the island.

For two years the colonists worked hard to supply all their needs.

They still kept watch, but no ship came near the island. They already knew, from Captain Nemo, that it was not shown on any chart or map of the Pacific Ocean. It had never been described in any book for seamen.

None of them expected to see anything during his time on watch.

So it was a great surprise when one day Herbert, from the window, called out: "Pencroft, my friend with the wonderful eyes, will you come and look at this? It could be a little cloud, but I think it might be smoke."

Pencroft joined his young friend at the window.

"You are right, Herbert. It *is* smoke."

After an hour it was possible to see that the smoke came from a steamship. It was coming straight towards the island. It was probably not necessary to follow Smith's plan, but the colonists decided to do so: a great cloud of smoke went up from a fire (helped by gunpowder) on top of the rock wall. And at the same time the American flag went up near the fire.

The ship was a British ship making charts for world shipping.

The captain of the *Surveyor* was glad to take the colonists, and even Top, to the nearest port.

Cyrus Smith and Gideon Spillet were glad to go. There was work for them to do in a quickly changing world.

Nab was glad to go – with his dear master.

Pencroft was delighted to be on a ship once more. He soon made himself useful, and he had a great number of new stories to tell to the other sailors.

Only Herbert was not sure. The boy – now a young man – wanted to see his mother and father again. But at the same time, he had grown to love the island life. Perhaps, he thought, the life for him was the life of an explorer – or of the captain of a ship like the *Surveyor*.

Questions

Questions on each chapter

1 *In the balloon*
   1 Where did the storm carry the balloon to?
   2 Why did they throw everything out?
   3 What happened to Cyrus Smith?
   4 Where did the others jump down from the balloon?

2 *The island*
   1 Where did Spillet want to go?
   2 What food did Herbert find?
   3 Why was Nab weeping?

3 *Cyrus Smith is found*
   1 What did Pencroft do every hour?
   2 Where did Top lead them?
   3 Where was Cyrus Smith?
   4 What did they see on the wet ground?
   5 What was Smith able to eat?

4 *Life on the island*
   1 Why did the colonists want bows and arrows?
   2 Which of them made cooking pots?
   3 How did Cyrus Smith open the lock?

5 *The box*
   1 What weapons were in the box?
   2 Who was pleased to find paper in the box?
   3 What did Pencroft want that was not in the box?

6 *The rock wall*
   1 Why were the colonists able to leave the fire?
   2 What was on the other side of the rock wall?
   3 Where did the water in the lake come from?

7 *Finding the cave*
   1 What was the passage going towards?
   2 What was at the bottom of the big hole?
   3 What did Herbert want to do?

8 *"Cave House"*
   1 What had the sea destroyed in the rock house?
   2 How did the colonists get things up to Cave House?
   3 What kind of lights did Smith want?
   4 Who told stories that were not always true?

9 *Pirates!*
   1 Who first saw the ship?
   2 What was the ship's flag?
   3 How did the colonists hide their windows?
   4 What was Bob Harvey?
   5 What happened to one of the windows?
   6 What happened to the pirates' ship?

10 *Torpedo!*
   1 What part of the ship had suffered most?
   2 Who found a piece of metal on the beach?
   3 What was the broken cylinder?

11 *The mysterious friend*
   1 What medicine did Herbert need?
   2 When did the mysterious "friend" help the colonists?
   3 Who was dying?

12 *Down the hole*
   1 Where was Pencroft when he shouted?
   2 How did the colonists go out over the water?

13 *Captain Nemo*
   1 What name did Smith call the man in the submarine?
   2 What was the name of the submarine?
   3 What was the captain's real name?
   4 What did he give to the colonists?

14 *Leaving the island*
   1 What was the work of the steamship?
   2 What did Herbert think he might like to do?

Questions on the whole story

These are harder questions. Read the Introduction, and think hard about the questions before you answer them. Some of them ask for your opinion, and there is no fixed answer.

1 The balloon:
    a Where did it come from?
    b Why were the four men and a boy in its basket?
    c Why did it go so far?
    d Why did they cut off the basket?

2 The island:
    a Where was the island?
    b How did these people arrive at the island:
        1 Cyrus Smith?
        2 the other colonists?
        3 Captain Nemo?

3 Who was the natural leader of the colonists? Why?

4 What was Gideon Spillet's work in America?

5 What was Pencroft's work before the story begins?

6 Which of the colonists do you like best? Why?

7 Read these quotations. Say who the speaker is in each one. Then answer the questions that follow each quotation.
    a "A ship! A ship!"
        1 Where is the speaker?
        2 What ship has he seen?
    b "We won't see him until he wants to be seen."
        1 Who does the speaker mean by "he" and "him"?
        2 When *do* the colonists see "him"?
    c "Does it matter what we have heard?"
        1 Where is the speaker?
        2 Who is he speaking to?

New words

anchor
a heavy metal object with points, lowered from a ship to the bottom of the sea on a rope to hold the ship in one place

bow
a piece of wood, bent by a string between the two ends. It shoots arrows.

bury
put (a dead body) into a hole in the ground

chart
a sailors' map of the sea

clay
heavy soil, soft when wet. It becomes hard when heated, and is used to make pots, etc

colonist
a person who has settled in a new country

crack
a narrow opening made by breaking

cylinder
a long round object, shaped like a round pencil but sometimes very much bigger

fiction
invented stories. **Science fiction** stories are not true but they use facts from science.

hook
a curved piece of metal for catching fish

mystery
something that you cannot understand or explain

pirate
a sea robber

shellfish
an animal that lives in water and has a hard outer case

submarine
a ship that travels under the water

torch
burning wood used as a light

torpedo
a long narrow machine that goes through the water to explode against a ship

weapon
something that you use to hurt or kill (for example, a gun or sword)